Detective McWoof

and the great
Poodle Doodler mystery

TOP SECRET

To Flora, with love. T.K.
For our beloved Olive. H.C-B.

OXFORD
UNIVERSITY PRESS

Great Clarendon Street, Oxford OX2 6DP

Oxford University Press is a department of the University of Oxford.
It furthers the University's objective of excellence in research, scholarship,
and education by publishing worldwide. Oxford is a registered trade mark of
Oxford University Press in the UK and in certain other countries

Text copyright © Timothy Knapman 2015
Illustrations copyright © Holly Clifton-Brown 2015

The moral rights of the author and illustrator have been asserted
Database right Oxford University Press (maker)

First published 2015

British Library Cataloguing in Publication Data
Data available

ISBN: 978-0-19-273995-7 (paperback)
ISBN: 978-0-19-273996-4 (eBook)

1 3 5 7 9 10 8 6 4 2

Printed in China

Paper used in the production of this book is a natural,
recyclable product made from wood grown in sustainable forests.
The manufacturing process conforms to the environmental
regulations of the country of origin.

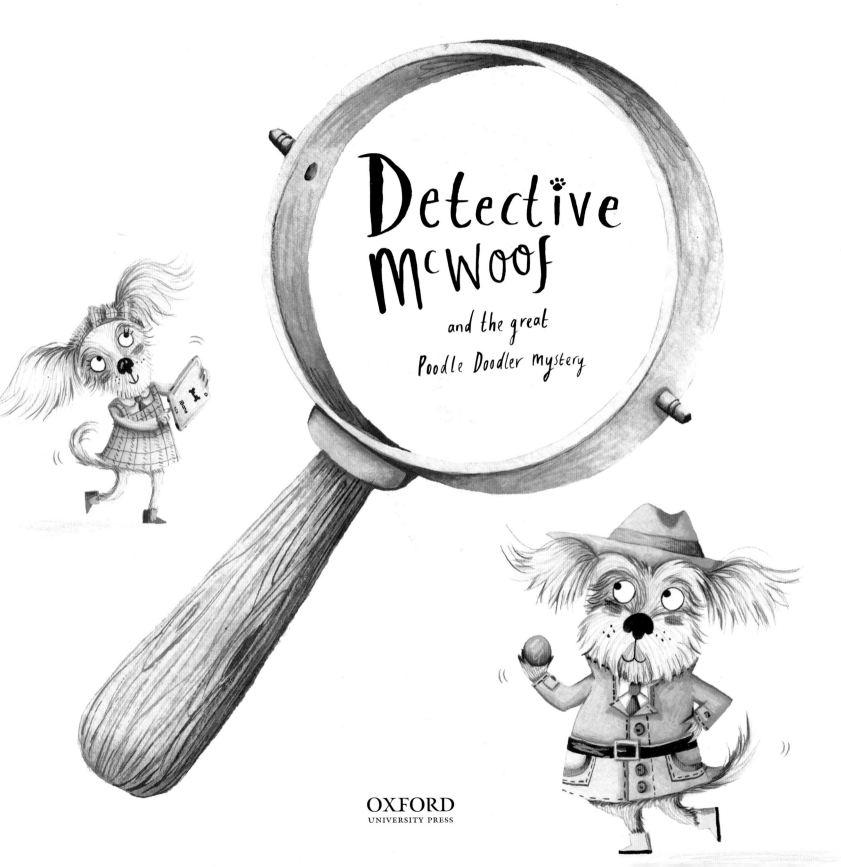

Detective McWoof

and the great
Poodle Doodler mystery

OXFORD
UNIVERSITY PRESS

WANTED
for barking
crimes

Detective McWoof and
Wanda were top dogs
at solving mysteries.

THE DAILY HOUND

CROSSWORD
MUZZLE

Bank
Robber
Gets
Collared!

Well, one of them was . . .

'Where's my lucky ball gone?'
said McWoof.

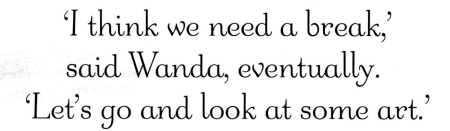

'I think we need a break,'
said Wanda, eventually.
'Let's go and look at some art.'

POODLE
DOODLER

At the gallery, McWoof stopped by a painting
by the famous artist Poodle Doodler.

'I don't understand modern art,' said McWoof.
'Is this painting the right way up?'

Then one of the guards ran in.
'Poodle Doodler has been DOGNAPPED!' he cried.

'Sounds like a case for us,' said McWoof.
'To the *Poochmobile*!'

McWoof and Wanda drove to Poodle Doodler's
place to sniff out some clues.

'Look, there goes my lucky ball!' said McWoof, suddenly.

He scampered
after the ball—
straight into the house.

'Nooooo!' yelled Wanda.
But it was too late.

'Look what you've done!'
said the butler.
'I'm calling the police.'

'No, wait,' said a voice . . .

It was Marilyn Mongrelle—Poodle Doodler's wife!
'The great Detective McWoof,' she said.
'If anyone can find my husband, it's you.'

Then she burst into tears.
Funny, though, Wanda spied
an onion in Marilyn's handkerchief...

Marilyn gave McWoof a tour of the house.
'I make these statues,' she said. 'I hope one day
they'll be as famous as my husband's pictures.'

'I still don't understand modern art,' said McWoof.
'Is that picture the right way up?'

'Now this statue *is* good,' he said.
'The eyes follow you round the room.'

POODLE DOODLER M.M

'While this is here, I like to think that
Poodle Doodler's still with us,' said Marilyn.

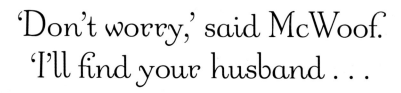

'Don't worry,' said McWoof.
'I'll find your husband . . .

'I'm on the trail
of the dognapper now!'

'Just as I thought,'
he cried.
'The butler did it!
Caught you red handed!'

'Ah,' said McWoof,
finally noticing
the mess he'd made.

'Get out now!'
barked the butler.

Over in
Mr Chow's Diner,
McWoof and Wanda
went through
the clues . . .

Clue One—the onion in
Marilyn's handkerchief.

Clue Two—the statue of Poodle Doodler whose eyes follow you round the room.

Clue Three—that picture McWoof thought was upside down. There was something odd about it, but what?

'We need to take another look
at that picture,' said Wanda.

But McWoof wasn't listening.

'Oh, look—there goes
my lucky ball,' he said.

And he was off again,
after that dratted ball!

Later that night, they slipped back into the mansion.

Maybe that picture *isn't* the right way up, thought Wanda.

'I think I've got it!' she cried.

'You've got my ball?' said McWoof.

'Stop going on about your ball,' said Wanda.
'Or somebody will hear us.'

'Too late,' said a voice . . .

It was Marilyn Mongrelle.

'Butler, stop those dogs!'
she said.

POODLE DOODLER M.M

'Not before I smash this statue,' cried Wanda.

'No!' yelled Marilyn. But it was too late.

Wanda pushed the statue over
and inside it they found . . .

Poodle Doodler!

'Thank you,' cried Poodle Doodler.
'You've rescued me at last!'

'But how did you know?'
said McWoof.

'The three clues, silly,'
said Wanda.

'The onion in Marilyn's handkerchief was there to make her cry. She was only pretending to be sad.

She wanted her husband out of the way, so she covered him in clay.

And Poodle Doodler was worried she was going to do it, which is why he painted this clue!'

'All right, so I did do it!'
said Marilyn.

'I just wanted Poodle Doodler
gone for a few days
so I could be the
famous one . . .

'But you'll never catch me!'

'After her!' cried McWoof.

But just at that moment . . .

McWoof's ball came bouncing up behind Marilyn and bonked her on the head.

'I told you it was
my lucky ball,'
said McWoof.

Marilyn was famous at last.
It was all over the news
when she got sent to jail.

To say thank you for freeing him,
Poodle Doodler painted pictures
of McWoof and Wanda.

THE HOUNDINGTON POST

MARILYN
MONGRELLE
ARREST!

HOUNDSTOWN HALL

WOOF & WASH

'I owe it all
to Wanda,'
said McWoof.

'And my lucky ball here,
of course . . .

'Oops!

After it!'